Health Solutions
Diabetes

Edited by
Dr Savitri Ramaiah

STERLING PAPERBACKS
An imprint of
Sterling Publishers (P) Ltd.
A-59, Okhla Industrial Area, Phase-II,
New Delhi-110020.
Tel: 26387070, 26386209; Fax: 91-11-26383788
E-mail: sterlingpublishers@airtelmail.in
ghai@nde.vsnl.net.in
www.sterlingpublishers.com

Diabetes
© 2008, Sterling Publishers (P) Ltd.
ISBN 978-81-207-3327-5
Reprint 2008, 2011, 2012

All rights are reserved.
No part of this publication may be reproduced, stored in a retrieval system or transmitted, in any form or by any means, mechanical, photocopying, recording or otherwise, without prior written permission of the original publisher.

Printed and Published by Sterling Publishers Pvt. Ltd.,
New Delhi-110 020.

Information for this series, has been provided by *Health Update*, a monthly bulletin of the Society for Health Education and Learning Packages. The Update is intended to provide you with knowledge to adopt preventive measures and cooperate with the doctor during illness for better outcome of treatment.

Contributors

Allopathy
Dr Savitri Ramaiah
(Member-Secretary, HELP and Editor, Health Update)

Ayurveda
Dr V N Pandey
(Former Director, Central Council for Research in Ayurveda and Siddha, New Delhi)

Homoeopathy
Dr Sangeeta Chopra
(Consultant Homoeopathy, New Delhi)

Nature Cure
Dr Sambhashiva Rao
(Consultant, Naturopathy, Pandrapadu, Dist. Guntur, Andhra Pradesh)

Unani
Hakim Mohammed Khalid Siddiqui
(Director, Central Council for Research in Unani, New Delhi)

Preface

Health Solutions is an easy-to-read reference series put together by *Health Update* and assisted by a team of medical experts who offer the latest perspectives on body health.

Each book in the series enhances your knowledge on a particular health issue. It makes you an active participant by giving multiple perspectives to choose from — allopathy, acupuncture, ayurveda, homoeopathy, nature cure and unani.

This book is intended as a home adviser but does not substitute a doctor.

The opinions are those of the contributors, and the publisher holds no responsibility.

Contents

Preface	4
Introduction	6
Allopathy	7
Ayurveda	84
Homoeopathy	91
Nature Cure	96
Unani	102

Introduction

Diabetes is a condition that alarms people. It causes apprehension about the quality of life. But almost all can lead a full, active life with regular control of their diet and medicines.

Diabetes is a disorder of the chemical reactions that are necessary for proper utilisation of carbohydrates, fats and protein from the diet along with inadequate or lack of insulin. Insulin is a hormone produced in the pancreas to regulate the amount of sugar in the blood.

Hereditary causes, obesity, age, sex, viral infection, injury, stress, sedentary life are some of the reasons for diabetes.

Allopathy

Diabetes mellitus, commonly called diabetes, is a condition that makes many people worry about the quality and longevity of their life after being told that they have diabetes. Anyone can get diabetes but almost all of them can lead a full, active life with regular control of their diet and medicines. About eighteen million people in India are suspected to have diabetes.

Diabetes is a disorder of the chemical reactions that are necessary for proper utilisation of carbohydrates, fats and protein from the diet along with inadequate or lack of *insulin*. In other words, diabetes results when the body cannot use some foods because of inadequate production of insulin. Insulin is a *hormone* produced in the *pancreas* to regulate the amount of blood in the sugar. Pancreas is an organ that is located behind the stomach as indicated in Figure 1. It has small groups of cells called the *Islets of Langerhans*. Inside these islets are specialised cells called *beta cells*. These beta cells produce insulin.

What is the role of insulin in our body?

All cells in your body need energy in order to function normally. This energy is derived from the food you eat which is made up of carbohydrates, proteins and fats. After digestion, the carbohydrate, which mainly comes from cereals and starch such as wheat, rice, fruit, etc., is converted into glucose, or simple sugar. This glucose is the main source of energy for all the body cells. Excess glucose is stored in the liver and muscles as a compound called *glycogen*.

The glucose enters the cells through *receptors*, which are proteins on the surface of the cells. All the hormones in the body can act on the target cells only after they attach to the receptors. Thus, the glucose can enter the cells only if the insulin, which is a hormone, attaches itself to the receptors on the cell wall. When the insulin is either inadequate, absent, or abnormal, it is difficult for the glucose to enter the cells and provide energy.

In addition to helping glucose enter the cells and providing them with energy, insulin is also involved in storage of glycogen in the liver and muscles. Thus, it is involved in storage of reserve energy. In between meals when the cells need energy, glycogen is converted back into glucose and used by the cells.

Normally, pancreas releases insulin proportional to the amount of food you eat. The beta cells monitor blood glucose levels regularly and release the amount of insulin necessary to use the glucose in the blood. In diabetes, the pancreas either does not produce insulin or produces too little or produces defective insulin that cannot be used by the body. Thus, the blood glucose cannot be used effectively by the cells and excess glucose cannot be stored in the liver.

Diabetes can occur when there is either inadequate or lack of production of insulin or production of defective insulin by the pancreas. A schematic diagram of the mechanism through which pancreas blood sugar level is illustrated in Figure 1.

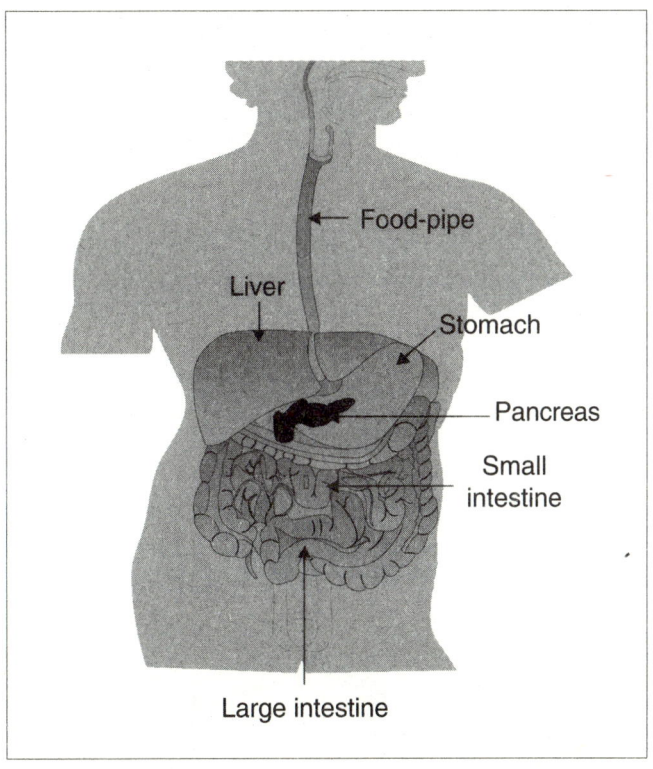

Fig 1: Location of the pancreas

What are the symptoms of diabetes?

There are three main symptoms of diabetes. These include:
- increased thirst,
- increased hunger and
- increased frequency of passing the urine.

You may also have some or all of the symptoms listed in Box 1.

Box 1: Symptoms of diabetes

- Increased frequency of passing the urine, including at night
- Excessive thirst
- Excessive hunger
- Feeling tired and weak most of the time
- Loss of weight
- Slow healing of cuts and wounds
- Numbness or tingling in the feet
- Skin infections
- Blurred vision
- Dry or itchy skin

Frequent passing of the urine and increased thirst

Kidneys filter about fifteen hundred litres of blood per day. They excrete some water and waste products as urine and absorb most of the filtered blood including glucose. If the blood has more glucose than what the kidneys can reabsorb, it passes out with the urine. As the glucose passes out of the body, it takes a lot of water along with it in order to flow easily out of the body. Increased water in the urine increases the frequency of passing urine, which in turn results in increased thirst.

Excessive hunger

When adequate insulin does not attach to the receptors, the cells in the body do not get any energy. They therefore send a message of "hunger" to the brain. The brain responds to this message by giving you a feeling of excessive hunger. Despite eating more, the glucose derived from the food cannot be used for energy as it passes out in urine.

Lack of energy in the cells results in general weakness and tiredness. Also, in the absence of insulin, the cells cannot derive any energy. Energy is therefore derived from the fat and muscles. When energy is derived from fats and muscles, you will lose weight, even if you eat enough to satisfy your hunger.

Skin problems

Excess blood sugar suppresses the body's natural defense mechanism. This is why cuts and wounds heal very slowly if there is high blood sugar. Also, sugar is a very good food for the bacteria to grow. Thus, skin infections are more common in diabetes. The skin, especially around genitals may be itchy.

What are the types of diabetes?

There are two main types of diabetes:

Type I or insulin dependent diabetes

About ten per cent people with diabetes have Type I diabetes. Their bodies do not produce any insulin and therefore regular insulin injections are necessary to maintain normal blood sugar.

Box 2: Type I and Type II diabetes		
Features	*Type 1 diabetes*	*Type II diabetes*
Other names	Insulin dependent diabetes, Juvenile diabetes	Non-insulin dependent diabetes, Adult onset diabetes
Age of onset	Usually below forty years	Normally above forty years
Body weight	Thin	Normally overweight
Symptoms	Appear suddenly	Appear slowly
Production of insulin	Absent	Inadequate or defective
Control of diabetes	Requires insulin injections	May be controlled with medicines. If not, insulin may be required.

Type II or non-insulin dependent diabetes

About eighty-five per cent people with diabetes have Type II diabetes. Their bodies produce some insulin but it is either inadequate or is defective.

Some of the major differences between Type I and Type II diabetes are listed in Box 2 and various types of diabetes are listed in Box 3.

Box 3: Types of diabetes

- Insulin dependent diabetes
- Non-insulin dependent diabetes mellitus
- Malnutrition related diabetes
- Due to diseases of the pancreas
- Due to protein deficiency

Diabetes associated with other conditions:

- Cancer of the pancreas
- Abnormalities of other hormones
- Due to medicines such as steroids
- Abnormalities of insulin or its receptors
- Some hereditary conditions

Malnutrition related diabetes

Diabetes among young people with severe malnutrition and starvation is called malnutrition-related diabetes. Although this condition leads to high blood sugar, some of the complications associated with other types of diabetes are absent. Insulin is necessary to control malnutrition related diabetes.

Gestational diabetes

Some women have high blood sugar during pregnancy. Diabetes during pregnancy is called gestational diabetes.

What are the predisposing factors of diabetes?

Predisposing factors are those that increase the risk of your getting a particular disease. There are many conditions that increase the risk of diabetes. Box 4 lists the most important predisposing factors.

Box 4: Predisposing factors of diabetes

- Hereditary
- Obesity
- Age
- Sex
- Pregnancy
- Viral infections
- Injury to the pancreas
- Stress
- Sedentary lifestyle

Hereditary

Blood relatives of people with diabetes are more likely to develop diabetes than those who do not have it in their family. The risk depends upon the number of family members who have diabetes. Higher the number of relatives with diabetes, greater is the risk. There is five per cent risk of your developing diabetes if your parents or siblings have diabetes. This risk may increase to fifty per cent if you are overweight.

Obesity

Almost eighty per cent people who develop diabetes later in life are overweight. Excess weight increases the body's demand for insulin. Obese adults have larger fat cells in their bodies. It is believed that large fat cells do not respond well to insulin. Symptoms of diabetes *may* disappear with loss of weight.

Age

The risk of diabetes increases with age, especially after forty years, mainly because the number of beta cells in the pancreas that produce insulin decrease as age advances.

Sex

Both men and women have the same risk of developing diabetes till early adulthood. After thirty years, women are at higher risk as compared to men. Women who develop diabetes during pregnancy are at higher risk of developing Type II diabetes later in life.

Viral infections

Some viral infections may destroy the beta cells in the pancreas and therefore cause diabetes.

Injury

An accident or injury that damages the pancreas may also destroy the beta cells, thus leading to diabetes.

Stress

Some hormones released during stress may block the effect of insulin on the cells, thus causing diabetes.

Sedentary lifestyle

Some recent studies have indicated that people with sedentary lifestyle are more likely to have diabetes as compared to those who lead an active life. It is believed that exercise and physical activity increases the effect of insulin on the cells.

How is diabetes diagnosed?

Diabetes can be diagnosed by blood and urine tests. In case of a routine check-up where you do not have any symptoms, your doctor is likely to suggest *random blood sugar test*. This means that your blood can be tested at any time of the day irrespective of when you have last eaten. In case diabetes is suspected, *fasting blood sugar* (after twelve hour fast) and *post-prandial blood sugar* levels are tested (two hours after food). Diabetes is diagnosed if your random blood sugar level is more than 200mg/100ml of blood and fasting blood sugar is more than 140mg/100ml.

Box 5: Interpretation of glucose tolerance test			
Timing of blood sample	Normal	*Impaired Glucose tolerance*	Diabetes
Fasting	<115	<140	140 or above
Two hours after taking glucose	<140	140-199	200 or above

Until some years ago, urine tests were routinely recommended for diagnosis of diabetes. However, it is not recommended anymore because several other health conditions and medicines may give false positive results.

Glucose tolerance test

Occasionally, an oral glucose tolerance test is necessary to confirm diagnosis. This test, which indicates your body's capacity to use glucose, is performed in the morning after an overnight fast. You should have had normal diet for three days before taking the test. In this test, blood for measuring fasting blood sugar level is first taken. Next, you will be given seventy-five grams of glucose. Blood samples are taken half an hour, one hour and two hours after taking glucose. The results of glucose tolerance test are interpreted as normal, impaired glucose tolerance and diabetes. Impaired glucose tolerance test is considered to be a risk factor for future diabetes. It however is not included in the diagnosis of diabetes. The blood sugar levels for each of these conditions is listed in Box 5.

Glucose tolerance test is not recommended for people who are either on bed rest or are suffering from some diseases, especially infections.

What are the complications of diabetes?

Complications of diabetes can be either *acute* because of insulin deficiency, which increases blood sugar to very high levels and *chronic* because of changes in the blood vessels of various parts of the body.

Acute complications include diabetic ketoacidosis and repeated infections.

Diabetic ketoacidosis or coma

When insulin levels are low, the body cannot use glucose for energy and therefore body fats are mobilised from their stores. The breakdown of fats to release energy results in formation of *fatty acids*. These fatty acids pass through the liver and form a group of chemical compound called *ketones*. Ketones are excreted in the urine. Presence of ketones in the urine is called *ketonuria*.

Increased level of ketones in the body tissues is called *ketosis*. Ketosis may increase acidity of the body fluids and tissues to abnormally high levels and cause a condition called *acidosis*. Acidosis as a result of increased ketones is called *ketoacidosis*. Box 6 lists the symptoms of ketoacidosis.

Diabetic ketoacidosis is an emergency condition, and if not treated on time, can cause death. Appropriate dose of insulin and intravenous fluids can reverse diabetic ketoacidosis. In case you have

---

Box 6: Complications of diabetes

Acute
1. Ketoacidosis. Symptoms include:
   - Dehydration as indicated by dryness in the mouth and loss of elasticity of the skin
   - Fruity smell of breath
   - Nausea, vomiting and pain in the abdomen
   - Deep breathing
   - Increased rate of breathing
   - Severe weakness, drowsiness that can lead to unconsciousness or coma
2. Infections

Chronic
- Coronary artery disease — blood vessels of the heart affected. Heart diseases such as heart attack and angina may therefore occur.
- Nephropathy — kidney functions affected
- Neuropathy — nerves in various parts of the body affected
- Retinopathy — Retina of the eyes mainly affected. Partial or complete loss of vision may occur.

symptoms suggestive of ketoacidosis, you can take the following measures until you reach the hospital.
- Increase regular insulin dose by at least twenty per cent;
- Drink as much fluids as possible; and
- Get urine tested for ketones and blood for glucose levels every four to six hours.

Infections

People with diabetes are more likely to have infections because of three main reasons: (a) bacteria grow very well if blood glucose levels are high; (b) natural defense mechanism of people with diabetes is low and (c) associated complications of diabetes increase the risk of infections.

Common infections among people with diabetes include skin infections, urinary tract infections, diseases of the gums, tuberculosis and some fungal infections.

Chronic complications are more common if normal blood sugar levels are not maintained regularly. People with diabetes are more likely to have diseases of the heart, blood vessels, kidneys, eyes and the nerves.

Diseases of the heart and the blood vessels

Atherosclerosis is a condition in which there is (a) hardening of the arteries and (b) narrowing of the arteries due to deposits of fat in its inner lining. It is a slowly progressive disease. It however develops faster in people with diabetes. This is why diabetics are twice more likely to have heart attack or angina as compared to non-diabetics. They are also at higher risk of developing high blood pressure.

Hardening of the arteries of the legs can affect the leg muscles because of reduced blood supply. This may result in cramps, discomfort or weakness while walking. If the blood supply to the leg is greatly reduced or cut off for a long time, there may be death of the tissues. If this happens, the affected part may have to be cut off to save life.

Damage to the kidneys

Diabetes can affect small blood vessels of the kidneys. As a result, the efficiency of the kidneys to filter waste products is adversely affected. Adverse kidney functions result in excretion of a protein called *"albumin"* in the urine. Damage to the kidneys may continue to deteriorate, especially if blood sugar levels are not under control. Kidney damage due to diabetes is more common in Type I diabetes as compared to Type II diabetes.

Damage to the eyes

People with diabetes are more likely to have partial or complete loss of vision as compared to those without diabetes.

Damage to the nerves

Almost seventy per cent people with diabetes have varying degrees of nerve damage. Damage to the nerves is called *neuropathy*. Neuropathy as a result of diabetes is called *diabetic neuropathy*.

High blood sugar destroys nerve fibres and a layer of fat around the nerves. Damaged nerves cannot pass the signals to and from the brain properly. As a result, you may either have loss of sensation, increased sensation or pain in the affected parts. Damage to the nerves on the periphery of the body is more common than in other parts of the body. The damage normally starts from the toes, and progresses to feet and legs. This can lead to numbness, tingling sensation, burning, dull pain, stabbing pain or cramps. The skin may become so sensitive that even pressure from the shoes and clothes may not be tolerated.

How can complications of diabetes be prevented?

You can prevent complications of diabetes through the following seven measures:

- Always maintain good control over blood sugar levels.
- Maintain normal blood pressure. If you have high blood pressure, take medicines prescribed by your doctor regularly.
- If you are obese, reduce your weight through proper diet control and regular exercise.
- Reduce intake of fats and cholesterol in your diet.
- Develop a routine of regular exercise *after* consulting with your doctor.
- Do not smoke.

- Get regular general check-up done in order to detect complications of diabetes, if any, at the earliest.

What is the treatment for diabetes?

Diabetes cannot be cured but can be controlled through several ways. These mainly include insulin, medicines, diet control and exercises. Management options for diabetes depend upon the type of diabetes and its severity. Box 7 lists the main aims of treatment of diabetes.

Box 7: Aims of treatment of diabetes

- To achieve best blood sugar level that is appropriate for you.
- To provide relief from symptoms of diabetes.
- To balance diet, exercise and medicines or insulin.
- To reduce risk factors associated with complications such as obesity, smoking, high cholesterol and high blood pressure.
- To ensure normal growth among children and young adults who have diabetes.
- To maintain normal body weight.
- To prevent acute complications such as ketoacidosis and infections.
- To prevent, if possible, or else detect at the earliest and manage chronic complications.

What is the treatment for Type I diabetes?

A regimen of insulin injections, diet and exercise are recommended for management of Type I diabetes. Insulin can only be given as an injection. This is because insulin is a protein and if taken orally, it is broken down during digestion and destroyed.

What are the types of insulin?

There are several types of insulin. All these types differ in three major characteristics: (a) when it begins its action on the body cells after injection, (b) when it reaches the peak activity and (c) the duration for which its action lasts. Based on these criteria, insulin injections can be grouped as short-acting, intermediate acting or long-acting.

The peak action of short-acting insulin is about one to three hours and the action lasts for four to eight hours. Intermediate-acting insulin reaches peak action within four to six hours and its action lasts for eight to twelve hours. Long-acting human insulin reaches peak within four to eight hours and its action lasts for eight to fourteen hours.

Short-acting insulins are also known as *soluble* or *regular* insulin. It is transparent in appearance.

Intermediate-acting insulin includes *NPH* (Neutral Protamine Hagedorn) and *Lente insulin*. NPH is a modified insulin that contains small amount of *protamine*, one of a group of simple proteins. Its action begins early and effect lasts for intermediate duration.

Lente insulin, which is made from ultralente and semi-lente insulin, has the same characteristics as NPH insulin.

Long-acting insulin include *protamine zinc insulin* and *ultralente*. They have prolonged duration of action. These insulins are not commonly used for treatment of diabetes.

In recent times, *pre-mixed insulins* are available and are preferred. These contain short-and intermediate-acting insulins. Pre-mixed insulins avoid the likely risk of manually mixing incorrect doses of more than one type of insulin. They are however recommended only if blood sugar levels are under good control.

Earlier, insulin was extracted from the pancreas of some animals. In recent times, however, bio-synthetic insulin is also available that is similar to human insulin. Although human insulin is expensive, it is preferred because it greatly reduces the risk of complications such as *insulin resistance.*

Human insulin is prepared by copying and putting the human *gene* (the basic unit of genetic material) that codes for insulin protein inside a bacteria. Several techniques are employed on this gene to make the bacteria want to use it so that insulin is made by it regularly. The insulin from the bacteria is then converted into human insulin through sophisticated techniques. Human insulin is also prepared by using yeast cells instead of bacteria.

When is insulin recommended for control of diabetes?

Insulin is recommended for five main conditions:
- Diabetes among children
- Diabetes among people who are underweight and malnourished
- Tendency to develop ketoacidosis among diabetics
- In emergencies such as surgery, pregnancy, high fever, or diabetic coma
- If other methods of blood sugar level such as medicines, diet and exercise have not been effective.

What are the insulin injection regimens?

Several insulin regimens are used to treat different people with insulin dependent diabetes. Your doctor will choose the regimen most suited to you based on (a) your blood sugar levels, (b) desired degree of diabetic control, (c) extent to which the insulin produced by the pancreas can fill the gap left by the insulin injections, (d) your lifestyle and (e) ability to adjust to insulin injections.

Once-daily injections, even if it is mixture of short and delayed action insulins cannot achieve desired insulin levels throughout the day among those who have little or no insulin being produced by the body. *Twice daily mixed insulins* is the simplest and most commonly used regimen. It aims to provide (a) background and midday meal insulin requirement with an intermediate action insulin and (b) cover the two main meals of the day (breakfast and evening meal) with short-acting insulin. Both insulins are injected before breakfast and evening meal.

Normally, about two-thirds of total daily insulin requirement is given in the morning and remaining one-third in the evening. The ratio of short- and intermediate-acting insulin normally differs in the morning and evening. Your doctor will recommend the desired ratio and dose based on the results of blood sugar measurements throughout the day. If insulin regimen is not well regulated, blood sugar levels may fall below normal, especially between meals and early in the morning.

What is the correct method of taking insulin injection?

Your doctor is the best person to advise you on the correct method of taking insulin injections. The information included here may be used as a guideline or reference.

If you **use one type of insulin**:
1. Wash your hands. Turn the insulin bottle on its side and roll it between your palms to mix it. Do not shake the bottle.
2. Wipe the top of the insulin bottle clean.
3. Pull the plunger of the injection syringe to draw in air equal to your insulin dose in units.
4. Push the needle through the top of the bottle and inject air into the bottle.

5. With the needle in the bottle, turn it upside down and pull the plunger to fill the syringe just beyond the marking of your dose of insulin.
6. Carefully and slowly, push the plunger till the marking line of the correct dose of your insulin.
7. Check for air bubbles. If they are present, gently tap the injection syringe so that the bubbles rise to the top. Repeat steps 5 and 6 above and check for bubbles again. Continue these two steps till there are no air bubbles in the injection syringe.
8. Remove the needle from the bottle.
9. Wipe and clean the area where you want to take insulin injection. Some people prefer to clean the injection site with a cotton swab dipped in alcohol. This is not always essential.
10. Hold a large pinch of skin between your thumb and fingers. If you do not do it, you may inject insulin into the muscle, especially if there is little fat below the skin.
11. Push the needle straight into the skin or at a slight angle.
12. Pull out the needle and wipe the injection site clean.

If you **use more than one type of insulin:**
1. Wash your hands and wipe the tops of both the insulin bottles clean.
2. Turn the bottle containing intermediate or longer-acting insulin such as NPH or Lente insulin upside down and roll between your hands to mix it. Do not shake it.

3. Pull plunger of the syringe to draw in air equal to your dose of NPH or Lente insulin.
4. Push the needle through the top of the NPH or Lente insulin bottle and inject the air into the bottle.
5. Remove the empty syringe and needle from the bottle.
6. Pull the plunger to draw in air equal to the dose of your regular or plain insulin. Push the needle through the top of the regular insulin bottle and inject air into the bottle.
7. With the needle in the bottle, turn it upside down and pull the plunger to fill the syringe just beyond the mark of your dose or regular insulin. Push the plunger slowly up to the line of your correct dose of regular insulin.
8. Check for air bubbles. If they are present, gently tap the syringe so that they come to the top of the syringe. Repeat steps 7 and 8 and check for bubbles again. Repeat these steps till there are no bubbles.
9. Remove the needle from the bottle with regular insulin and push it through the top of the bottle containing NPH or Lente insulin.
10. Carefully pull the plunger back till the mark of your total dose of insulin.
11. Inject the dose of insulin as detailed in steps 9-12 for taking one type of insulin.

Where is insulin injection taken?

Suitable sites for insulin injection include lower abdomen, upper outer arm, upper outer thighs, and buttocks. Avoid injecting insulin near joints or bony areas. Injection sites are normally rotated to avoid formation or "lumps".

It is important that you learn to inject insulin yourself rather than depend on others in order to become more self-reliant. It will also allow flexibility in your normal day to day activities and routine.

What are the devices to inject insulin?

Devices for giving insulin are:

Insulin syringes

These are special injection syringes that are available in several sizes, such as 30 units, 50 units and 100 units. *It is important to remember that you should use the size of the syringe that corresponds to your insulin dose.* For example, if your dose is 40 units and you use a 50 units size of syringe, you will not be able to measure 40 units exactly. Avoid buying bulk disposal insulin syringes, either from India or from abroad as they may not be suited for the changes made in the insulin dose after you have bought the syringes.

Insulin pens

This device minimises the inconvenience of injections and may also improve the accuracy of insulin delivery. It holds a pre-filled cartridge of the desired type of insulin and has a disposable needle that can be changed for each injection. In some pens, you need to give the correct dose by pressing the plunger repeatedly after the needle is pushed into the injection site. Each time you press the plunger, a fixed dose of insulin is injected. In some other types of pen, you need to dial the correct dose of insulin before the injection. This withdraws the plunger with the part that has insulin. After you have inserted the needle in the injection site, you need to push the plunger to deliver the dose you had adjusted in the pen.

If the needle is left on the pen between injections, air may enter the part of the pen that contains the insulin. This can slow the delivery of the dose and so cause wastage of insulin after the needle is withdrawn. It is therefore important that you learn the correct technique of using the pens from your doctor.

Jet injectors

These devices are designed to eject insulin as a spray of small drops under such high pressure that these small drops enter the skin. These devices are not very popular because the absorption of insulin into the body may not always be uniform. They may also cause bruises at the site of giving insulin.

External insulin pump therapy

A portable insulin pump is an alternative method of injecting insulin that allows an intermediate dose of insulin to be given at any time of the day or for pre-programming changes in the rate of insulin delivery throughout the day. It has a small portable pump with an *infusion* set that ends in a needle or *cannula*. Infusion means a slow injection of a liquid into a vein or under the skin. Cannula is a hollow tube designed for putting into a body cavity such as blood vessel. The needle or cannula is put below the skin and changed once in twenty-four to seventy-two hours.

To take full advantage of external insulin pump therapy, you need to do self monitoring of blood sugar level several times a day and then make adjustments on the insulin dose as recommended by your doctor.

The main advantage of external insulin pump therapy is improved flexibility in matching insulin with variations in your schedule. It also helps to make necessary changes in the rate of insulin delivery at all times, especially in between meals. The main disadvantage of external insulin pump is the possibility of infections at the site of infusion. It has a higher risk of developing ketoacidosis because of interruption in insulin flow.

Implanted insulin pump therapy

In this option, small pumps that can be controlled from outside are put inside the abdomen. Insulin is released into the space around the organs of digestive system inside the abdomen. The insulin thus released is absorbed directly into the various organs. This method seems to reduce the risk of low blood sugar while trying to maintain normal blood sugar levels throughout the day. More research is needed before this technique can be recommended for control of diabetes.

Disposal of insulin syringes and needles

It is desirable that you collect old syringes and needles in special containers for sharp objects. Whenever you visit a major hospital, request someone handling wastes to dispose your syringes and needles along with those of the hospital. Improper disposal of needles and syringes can be dangerous for those handling them in the municipal bins.

What are the complications of insulin injections?

There are four main complications of insulin injections. These include (a) low blood sugar, (b) insulin allergy and resistance, (c) local reactions at injection site and (d) swelling of the body.

Low blood sugar

This is the most common complication of insulin injections. Box 8 lists the factors that lead to low blood sugar. Until you achieve good control over blood sugar levels, you may have two to three mild to moderate *insulin reactions.* Insulin reaction is a condition where the normal blood sugar level falls below normal. The normal blood sugar level is between 60-120 mg/100 ml. You may have insulin reaction in any of the following three conditions:
- The blood sugar level falls below 60mg/100ml;
- Blood sugar falls rapidly from high level to low level; or
- Blood sugar falls below your normal level.

Box 8: Causes of low blood sugar during insulin therapy

- Inaccurate self monitoring of blood glucose.
- Changes in the timing of meals and snacks.
- Changes in the type and quantity of food taken during meals and snacks.
- Changes in insulin absorption.
- An acute illness, especially if nausea and vomiting is present.
- A chronic illness that reduces insulin requirements. For example, inadequate functioning of kidneys, liver.
- Loss of weight
- Drinking alcohol
- Pregnancy
- Changes in the exercise or normal day-to-day activities.

An insulin reaction is the body's response to low blood sugar. Whenever there is low blood sugar, the brain releases some hormones that cause paleness, sweating, increased heart beat, irritability, etc. These hormones also release sugar stored in the liver as glycogen. Released glycogen increase blood sugar levels. Box 9 lists the symptoms of insulin reaction.

Box 9: Symptoms of insulin reaction

- Sweating and a cold, clammy feeling
- Numbness or tingling in lips or fingertips
- Dizziness, weakness
- Difficulty in speaking or slurred speech
- Palpitations or pounding heart
- Increased heart rate
- Increased irritability
- Nervousness
- Headache
- Blurred vision
- Hunger
- Pale skin
- Convulsions

Treatment

Whenever you have the symptoms of insulin reaction, do not wait to see if they go away on their own. Eat some sugar or candies immediately. It is desirable that you keep sugar with you all the time. You should also stop all activities and sit or lie down in order to reduce the body's demand for energy and therefore sugar. In case the symptoms persist for more than ten or fifteen minutes, have some sugar again. Avoid eating continuously till the symptoms disappear or eating whatever food is available as it will prevent blood sugar levels from stabilising.

Prevention

You can prevent insulin reaction by eating meals at fixed time every day, avoiding sudden changes in diet, exercise or insulin dose and eating a light snack before doing exercises. *It is important to carry a diabetic card with information about your diabetes condition so that others around can help you seek immediate medical help.*

Sometimes, high blood sugar and ketoacidosis may occur after taking excessive insulin. This type of rebound high blood sugar is called *Somyogi phenomenon*. It occurs due to release of some chemical compounds in the body as a result of low blood sugar. Somyogi phenomenon may be responsible for worsening of diabetes.

Formation of lumps

Sometimes, a firm round lump may form at the site of repeated insulin injection. The absorption of insulin from these lumps may not be complete. This complication is not commonly observed in those who take human insulin injections because they are more than ninety-eight per cent pure.

Insulin allergy and resistance

Insulin allergy is also not a common complication in those who use purified insulins, especially human insulins. Allergic reaction to insulin injection may be either at the site of injection or all over the body. Local reactions result in hardness, itching, red discolouration or pain at the injection site. The symptoms normally appear after thirty minutes to four hours after taking insulin and are first observed within the first week or month after starting insulin treatment. Insulin allergy disappears after some time.

Insulin resistance is a condition in which *antibodies* are formed in the body in response to insulin injections. Antibodies are special kinds of blood protein that are produced in response to a foreign or disease causing agent.

The most common cause of insulin resistance is obesity. It may also be due to periodic stress and illness. Insulin resistance in people who are not overweight may be due to antibodies to insulin, abnormalities in the insulin receptors, increased local destruction of insulin or secretion of abnormal insulin.

Insulin resistance is a condition in which the more than two hundred units of insulin are required to control blood sugar for several days. This demand should not be because of ketoacidosis, infection or some associated diseases of the *endocrine glands*. Endocrine glands are ductless glands that produce one or more hormones and secrete them directly in the blood stream.

Swelling

Insulin may rarely cause swelling of the body.

What is non-insulin dependent diabetes?

Non-insulin dependent diabetes, as the name suggests, is a condition where insulin injections are not essential to maintain normal blood sugar levels. It is also called *"Type II diabetes"*. Sometimes, insulin may be necessary to control blood sugar levels in people who have this type of diabetes especially if maximum doses of medicines have not been effective. Non-insulin dependent diabetes is more common in people above forty years and who are obese.

Non-insulin dependent diabetes can occur when either the pancreas produces inadequate insulin or the insulin is defective. Insulin is necessary for effective utilisation of glucose by the cells for energy. This is because insulin attaches itself to specialised proteins called *receptors* on the cell walls and act as gateways for glucose to enter the cells. Defective insulin cannot attach to these specialised proteins.

What are the causes of non-insulin dependent diabetes?

There are several causes of non-insulin dependent diabetes. Detailed below are some of the important ones.

Hereditary factors

Non-insulin dependent diabetes is five times more common among people whose blood relatives have diabetes as compared to those who do not have diabetes in their families. This risk increases to fifty per cent in case of obesity.

Increased storage of energy in the body is considered advantageous among people who have unpredictable food supply, especially among those who live in harsh conditions. However, if food is readily available, increased storage of energy in the body can lead to obesity, insulin resistance and perhaps non-insulin dependent diabetes. This perhaps explains why this type of diabetes is more common among people who adopt westernised lifestyles.

Obesity

Sedentary lifestyle of the urbanised society and excessive energy intake increases the risk of developing non-insulin dependent diabetes. The risk of developing diabetes decreases by six per cent for every five hundred kilo-calories used through exercise every day. It is believed that the distribution of fat in different parts of the body as well as the total fat in the body are important for determining the risk of developing non-insulin dependent diabetes. People who have excessive fat in the trunk region, especially if it is within the abdomen, are more likely to develop non-insulin dependent diabetes. This is because fat in the organs of the abdomen appears to be broken down for energy more easily. When fats are broken down for energy, the level of *fatty acids* in the blood increases. Increased fatty acids in the blood increase resistance to insulin through their action on the liver and muscles.

Malnutrition

It is believed that children who have malnutrition during the critical stages of development in the mother's uterus or during their first year of life are more likely to develop non-insulin dependent diabetes later in life. This is perhaps because inadequate nutrition, especially inadequate protein in the first few months after birth may cause irreversible damage to the *beta cells* in the islets of Langerhans. Since these beta cells secrete insulin, damage to them can result in inadequate production of insulin later in life.

Medicines

Prolonged intake of medicines such as steroids or some medicines for controlling high blood pressure can cause non-insulin dependent diabetes.

Other causes

Non-insulin dependent diabetes can also occur during pregnancy, or as a result of some diseases of other *endocrine glands*. Endocrine glands are ductless glands of the body that secrete hormones.

How does non-insulin dependent diabetes develop?

Figure 2 illustrates the probable mechanism of development of non-insulin dependent diabetes. It is important to remember that the process of development of non-insulin dependent diabetes may take several years. This process may also be reversed. About twenty-five per cent people with impaired glucose tolerance are likely to develop non-insulin dependent diabetes within five years. About fifty per cent people continue to remain in the category of impaired glucose tolerance and the remaining twenty-five per cent may go back to normal glucose tolerance. This reversal is more common among those who have lost weight and/or increased physical activity.

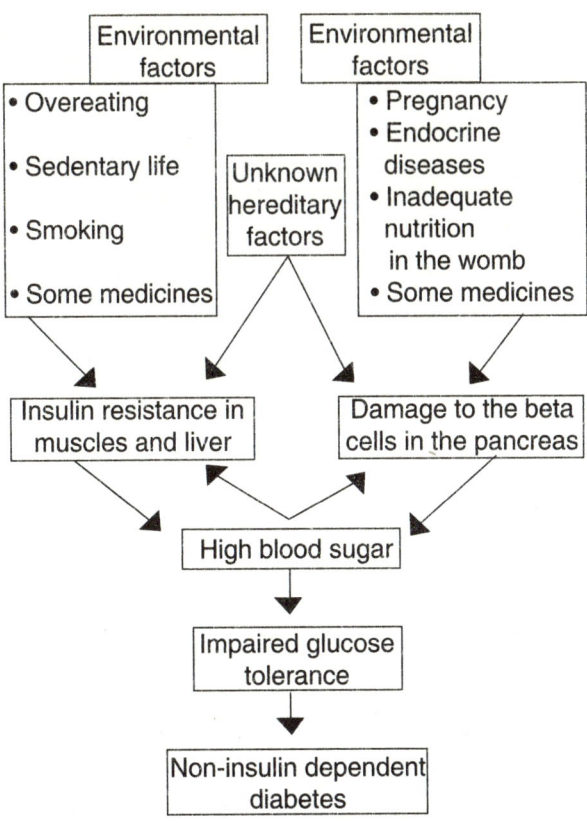

Fig 2. Probable mechanism of development of non-insulin dependent diabetes

What are the symptoms of non-insulin dependent diabetes?

Many people with diabetes may not have any symptoms. It may be diagnosed during routine investigations for skin infections or vision defects. Typical symptoms of diabetes include increased frequency of passing urine, excessive thirst and/or hunger, continuous weakness or tiredness, slow healing of cuts and wounds, numbness or tingling in the feet, skin infections and blurring or loss of vision.

What is the treatment for non-insulin dependent diabetes?

Just as for treatment of insulin-dependent diabetes, there are four main aims of management of non-insulin dependent diabetes. These include:

1. To provide relief from symptoms of diabetes and prevent acute complications of diabetes such as *ketoacidosis* and coma;
2. To reduce the risk of chronic complications such as damage to the eyes, kidneys, nerves or increased risk of heart diseases;
3. To increase life expectancy proportional to those who do not have diabetes; and
4. To restore quality of life to normal.

There are three approaches to management of non-insulin dependent diabetes. These include (a) diet, (b) exercise and (c) medicines.

What are benefits of reduced calorie intake in non-insulin dependent diabetes?

Weight loss is associated with immediate and long-term benefits in people with non-insulin dependent diabetes ,which are listed in Box 10.

Moderate restriction in daily intake of calories results in reduced blood sugar levels for most people and therefore the symptoms improve within a few days or weeks. This is because reduced calories result

> **Box 10: Benefits of weight loss in non-insulin dependent diabetes**
>
> *Benefits of short-term restriction in calorie intake without significant weight loss:*
> - Reduced glucose output from the liver
> - Fall in blood glucose levels
> - Relief from symptoms of diabetes
>
> *Benefits of long-term restriction in calorie intake with significant weight loss:*
> - Improved secretion of insulin
> - Enhanced sensitivity of the body cells to insulin
> - Further fall in blood sugar level
> - Fall in blood pressure
> - Reduced risk of developing thrombosis (an abnormal condition of the arteries where blood clots from on its inner layer thus reducing or stopping blood from the affected part)
> - Increased life expectancy
> - Reduced risk of faster progress of atherosclerosis (deposition of yellow plaques of cholesterol and fats, etc., on the inner linking of the arteries, thus making it narrower and harder)

in rapid decrease in the abnormally high output of glucose from the liver. It is believed that glucose output of the liver is reduced by two main mechanisms:

1. Increased utilisation of insulin by the liver; and
2. Suppression of glucose in the liver by *ketones*. Ketones are chemical compounds that are formed in the liver when fats are broken down to release energy whenever there is inadequate calorie intake. This is why blood levels of ketones increase during weight loss.

Continued dietary restriction that results in weight loss results in further beneficial effects on the body's ability to use glucose for energy. Weight loss has other benefits also, especially for those with non-insulin dependent diabetes. These include:

1. Reduced risk of developing ischaemic heart disease and therefore heart attack and angina;
2. Reduced blood pressure; and
3. Reduced level of "bad" cholesterol and increased level of "good" cholesterol in the blood.

What are the dietary recommendations for management of non-insulin dependent diabetes?

Your doctor and/or dietician will recommend an ideal diet for management of your diabetes depending on several factors. These include your current eating habits, lifestyle, age, sex, occupation, blood cholesterol levels, presence of high blood pressure and other health problems, if any.

Several studies have indicated that obese people who maintain their weight use more energy than people with normal weight. This can happen as they consume more energy than normal. Detailed below are some effective approaches to reducing calorie intake and therefore losing weight.

Calculate your intake and use of energy

If your weight is steady, your doctor and/or dietician will first estimate the amount of daily energy intake using standard formula. One such approach is described in Box 11.

Box 11: Formula for estimating the amount of energy used during twenty-four hours

Basal metabolic rate (Kilocalories/day)		**Physical activity multiplier**	
	Men		
Age (years)		*Activity*	
18-30 (Weight x 0.063) + 2.896 x 240		Light	1.55
31-60 (Weight x 0.048) + 3.653 x 240	×	Moderate	1.79
>60 (Weight x 0.040) + 2.459 x 240		Heavy	2.10
	Women		
Age (years)		*Activity*	
18-30 (Weight x 0.063) + 2.036 x 240		Light	1.56
31-60 (Weight x 0.034) + 3.538 x 240	×	Moderate	1.64
>60 (Weight x 0.038) + 2.755 x 240		Heavy	2.82

It is assumed that you will at least undertake light activities. If not, 15% of total 24-hour energy expenditure needs to be reduced. For example, if you are a male of 50 years old, weighing 75 kgs, your total 24-hour energy expenditure will be about 2698 kcal in case light activities are undertaken and 2293 kcal if you are especially sedentary.

Desirable target body weight

Your doctor will recommend that you work towards an "acceptable range" of weight rather than your "ideal weight". These ranges are normally prepared for different age groups and sex with an aim to provide longest life expectancy. Most specialists recommend acceptable weight as per the *body mass index*. You can calculate your body mass index by dividing your weight in kilograms by the square of your height in metres.

Your weight is considered normal and you will be at lower risk of health problems if your body mass index is less than twenty-five. If your body mass index is between twenty-five and thirty, you will be considered as overweight and will have moderate risk of health problems. If your body mass index is more than thirty, you are obese and will have a high risk of health problems.

Predicting rate of weight loss

It is desirable that you avoid unreasonable expectations of slimming diets. An ideal weight loss is about one to two kilograms per month. You are also likely to maintain the lost weight for a longer time if you loose weight gradually and slowly.

Planning a suitable diet

Your doctor will recommend a high carbohydrate, high fibre and low-fat diet to induce and maintain weight loss. You may lose weight with such a diet even if your total calorie intake does not come down. If you do not consume adequate fibre in your diet, there is a risk of increased blood cholesterol levels, which in turn can worsen diabetes.

Figure 3 illustrates an approach for weight reducing diet in diabetes. Box 12 lists general guidelines for dietary intake in non-insulin dependent diabetes.

Box 12: General guidelines for dietary intake in non-insulin dependent diabetes

- Avoid biscuits, cake or other bakery products as snacks in between meals.
- Use fats and oils that are low in saturated fatty acids (such as olive oil, sunflower oil, corn oil, etc.).
- Drink large volumes of water, skimmed milk and other low-calorie beverages in between meals.
- Eat regular meals.
- Avoid fried and sweet foods.
- Increase intake of vegetables by two times in every meal.
- Have rice, chapati, bread, potato or other cereals as the main part of every meal.
- Drink water or sugar-free drinks whenever you are thirsty.
- Eat smaller portions of meat or eggs.
- Eat smaller portions of pulses.

Calculate your acceptable weight range (body mass index 20-25)

Calculate target weight loss after 3 months (desirable —1-2 kg/month)

Calculate your current energy intake using standard formula

Assess your and your family's eating pattern

Contributions to total energy intake

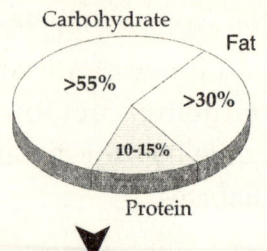

Prepare a diet plan:
- Reduce 500 kcal intake/day
- Modify eating behaviour
- Quit smoking
- Reduce alcohol intake
- Do exercise regularly

Regular review of:
- Body weight/body mass index
- Control of blood sugar
- Cholesterol level

Recommendations:
- Eat more of high fibre complex carbohydrates
- Limit sucrose (add <25g/day)
- Saturated fats to be <10% of total energy intake
- Consume mono-unsaturated fatty acids such as olive oil, rapeseed oil, etc.
- Limit salt intake if you have high blood pressure
- Limit alcohol intake
- Avoid foods that have high portion of artificial sweeteners.

Fig 3: An approach to weight reducing diet in diabetes

What is food exchange?

Food exchange is the process through which you can substitute an equivalent amount of calorie in the same group of food. For example, you can substitute one chapati with other cereals such as rice, potato or bread in the amount that give approximately the same calories as one chapati. The various groups for which exchange can be done are cereals, meat, milk and milk products, legumes and grams, fats and oils and fruits and vegetables.

Consistency in your diet is one of the most important factors for effective control of diabetes. This means that you need to consume approximately the same amount of carbohydrates, proteins and fats in each meal. The quantity of each of these foods will be based on your level of physical activity and schedule of insulin and/or medicines for diabetes. This means that the type of food you eat at different times is as important as the total calories you consume during the day.

You need to follow three rules for food exchange:
1. Substitute the food within the same meal.
2. Substitute correct amount of food exchanged.
3. Substitute from the same food group.

Box 13 lists some of the food exchanges for the Indian diet.

Box 13: List of food exchanges for the Indian diet

Cereal exchange: Each exchange contains 15g carbohydrates and 2g proteins. This amounts to about 70 calories.

- One chapati made from 20g atta
- Three tablespoons of cooked rice (75 g)
- One medium sized idli
- Half of medium sized potato
- One large slice bread
- 3/4th cup cooked porridge
- Three tablespoons cornflakes
- Two marie biscuits
- 1½ tablespoon ragi

Pulses and legumes exchange: Each exchange contains 15 g carbohydrates and 5g proteins. This amounts to 80 calories.

- One medium bowl cooked moong
- One medium bowl cooked Arhar
- One medium bowl cooked Chana dal
- One medium bowl cooked Rajma
- One medium bowl cooked lobia
- One medium bowl cooked urad

Meat exchange: Each exchange contains 7 g proteins and 5g fats. This amounts to about 75 calories.

- Chicken 30g
- One medium egg
- One inch cube of cheese
- Fish 30g
- Mutton 30g
- One piece paneer 1" x 1½"

Milk exchange: Each exchange consists of 12g carbohydrates, 8g proteins and 7g fats. This amount to about 145 calories.

- One glass toned milk (240ml)
- 250 ml of curds from toned milk
- 750 ml of butter milk
- 50g of paneer
- 3 tablespoons of skimmed milk

Fruit exchange: Each exchange consists of 10g carbohydrates. This amounts to about 40 calories.

• One medium orange • One small apple • One medium guava • ½ medium mango • 1 small pear • 2" slice papaya • 1 large slice watermelon • 1 glass tomato juice • 4 dry fruits (almonds, cashew, etc.) • 4 dates

Vegetables exchange: There are three groups of vegetable exchange.

100g vegetables in Group I give 20 calories.

• Cabbage • Spinach • Cauliflower • Capsicum • Bottle gourd • Brinjal • sarson ka saag • Tori

100g vegetables in Group II give about 32 calories.

• ladies finger • Onions • Radish • Carrot • Green peas • Beans • Pumpkin

25g vegetables in Group III give 20 calories.

• Potatoes • Sweet potato • Beetroot • Yam • Colocasia.

Fat/oil exchange: Each exchange contains about 5g fats, which amounts to about 45 calories.

• 1 teaspoon each of: Sunflower oil, Saffola, Soya oil, Til oil, Refined oil, Butter • 2 teaspoon of heavy cream

What is the role of exercise in management of diabetes?

Regular exercises play a very important role in the management of diabetes. This is because of the following main advantages:

1. Exercises help burn calories and therefore help reduce weight. Regular exercises can maintain acceptable weight.

2. Regular exercise can increase the number of receptors on the cell walls where the insulin can attach itself. This in turn can lead to increased utilisation of glucose by the cells for their energy.
3. Exercises improve blood circulation and tone the heart muscles.
4. Exercises increase good cholesterol and reduce the bad cholesterol levels.
5. Regular exercises can help relieve anxiety, stress and tension. It will therefore give a sense of well being.

Box 14: Guidelines for exercise in insulin dependent diabetes

- Monitor blood glucose levels before and after exercise.
- Avoid low blood sugar by:
  Taking extra carbohydrate before exercise and every hour in case exercise is for long duration. You should however avoid eating too much food before exercising.
- Avoid heavy exercise during the peak action of insulin.
- Take insulin injections in areas that will not be used for active exercises.
- Follow your doctor's advice for reducing insulin dose before undertaking strenuous or prolonged exercises.
- Blood glucose can fall even several hours after exercise. It is therefore important to check blood sugar periodically.

Starting an exercise routine

Before starting any exercise, it is important that you consult with your doctor first. This is because wrong type or duration of exercise can be harmful. For example, if you are taking insulin, any sport where reduced blood sugar levels can be dangerous need to

---

Box 15: Guidelines for exercise in non-insulin dependent diabetes

- Low blood sugar is not likely during exercises and therefore it may not be necessary to eat extra carbohydrates.
- Exercise to reduce weight need to be supported by reduced calorie intake.
- Moderate exercise needs to be done every day. Strenuous exercises may be done three times a week.
- It is important to include mild exercise for warming up and cooling down before and after an exercise respectively.
- Choose exercises that are most suited for your general health and lifestyle.
- Benefits of exercise are lost when no exercise is done for three continuous days.
- Exercise can increase appetite and therefore calorie intake. It is therefore important that you avoid eating extra food after exercises.
- The dose of oral medicines for diabetes may need to be reduced during regular exercise. Consult your doctor for adjusting the correct dose.

be avoided. These include diving, mountaineering, motor racing, sailing or rafting, etc. Similarly if the retina in your eye is damaged, strenuous exercises such as jogging can increase the risk of bleeding in the eyes and therefore loss of vision.

People with heart diseases, especially those who have non-insulin dependent diabetes need to consult with their diabetes doctor and cardiologist before starting any exercise routine. They will recommend exercises that have minimal risk of further damage to the heart and those that improve and tone the functions of the heart muscles. Similarly, people with damage to the nerves of the legs are at higher risk of having injuries in the feet and should therefore exercise with comfortable and well-fitting shoes.

General guidelines

It is desirable that you follow the following guidelines:
- As far as possible, exercise every day.
- It is not necessary that you undertake very strenuous exercises such as jogging. Even simple exercises such as walking will help burn adequate calories.
- Seek your doctor's help to plan exercises that are most suited for your needs and physical fitness.
- Use comfortable and well-fitting footwear that protect your entire feet.
- Avoid exercising in extreme heat or cold temperatures.

- Check your feet for any injuries after exercise every day.
- Avoid doing exercises when the blood sugar levels are not under good control.

Boxes 14 and 15 list the specific guidelines for exercise in insulin dependent and non-insulin dependent diabetes respectively.

What medicines are recommended for non-insulin dependent diabetes?

Non-insulin dependent diabetes may be treated with oral medicines, insulin injections or a combination of these. Oral medicines commonly used for treatment of diabetes include:

Sulphonylurea

This group of medicine has several medicines such as acetohexamide, chlorpropamide, glibenclamide, gliclazide, tolazamide, tolbutamide, etc. These medicines differ from one another mainly in the duration of their action and their recommended dose per day. For example, tolbutamide has a short-term effect and needs to be given two to three times a day. Chlorpropamide may act up to three days and its action may accumulate to severe levels if given every day. Glibenclamide is suitable for giving once a day in the morning.

Sulphonylureas are the first choice of medicines for management of non-insulin dependent diabetes. They stimulate the release of insulin by the beta cells of the islets of Langerhans in the pancreas. They however do not stimulate production of insulin.

There are few and generally mild side effects of these medicines. The most common adverse effect is uneasiness in the abdomen and diarrhoea. Some people may have skin rashes. Chlorpropamide has been reported to affect liver and may therefore cause jaundice. In excessive doses, medicines such as chlorpropamide and glibenclamide may cause excessive lowering of blood sugar.

Sulphonylurea is normally recommended thirty minutes before a meal in order to get best results in lower blood sugar levels two hours after meals.

Biguanides

An example of this group of medicines is Metformin. These medicines decrease absorption of carbohydrates and promote their *oxidation* in the tissues. Oxidation is a process by which the oxygen content of a chemical compound increases. Biguanides also reduce the conversion of fats and proteins into glucose in the liver.

Biguanides commonly produce unpleasant, bitter or metallic taste, loss of appetite, nausea and discomfort in the abdomen. You can reduce these side effects by taking the medicines with or just before meals. Biguanides may also result in lethargy, weakness of the muscles and excessive weight loss in some people. They are normally not recommended if you have heart, liver or kidney diseases.

> **Box 16. General precautions to be taken for oral medicines for diabetes**
>
> - In case you have acidity or other stomach disturbances, take the medicines with meals.
> - Your doctor may use these medicines with extra caution if you have heart, kidney or liver diseases.
> - Avoid drinking alcohol while on these medicines as it may react with the medicines and cause unpleasantness and flushing of the face.
> - Some medicines increases the action of sulphonylurea and it is therefore desirable that you avoid taking any medicines without consulting with your doctor.
> - Inform your doctor if you are pregnant as some medicines are not recommended during pregnancy.
> - In case you develop symptoms such as pain in the muscles, stop the medicine and consult your doctor immediately.
> - Stop taking the medicines in case allergic reactions develop.

Biguanides are normally recommended for people who are obese, are insulin resistant and have relatively less high blood sugar. It is given in combination with sulphonylurea if the latter does not control high blood sugar levels effectively.

Alpha-glucoside inhibitors

An example of this group of medicines is acarbose. It delays absorption of carbohydrates from the intestines and is normally recommended for those who have high carbohydrate intake. It is also sometimes recommended for obese people who do not follow the recommended diet for diabetes.

Acarbose may result in malabsorption in high doses. It may also result in mild side effects such as increased gas in the stomach, a feeling of bloating sensation in the abdomen and diarrhoea.

Box 16 lists the common precautions you may need to take for oral medicines for diabetes.

When is insulin recommended for management of non-insulin dependent diabetes?

If the non-insulin dependent diabetes is not controlled effectively by sulphonylurea, your doctor is likely to either recommend adding metformin or starting insulin therapy. Several studies have indicated that a combination of intermediate-and short-acting insulin given before breakfast and dinner is effective in people who do not respond satisfactorily to treatment with sulphonylurea.

There are several options for insulin regimens for management of non-insulin dependent diabetes. These may be either alone or in combination with oral medicines. Major options include:

- Premixed, short-and intermediate-acting insulin, twice a day;
- Multiple insulin injections (short-acting insulin before meals and NPH insulin at bedtime);

- Combination of NPH insulin in the morning and at bedtime and oral medicines such as sulphonylurea during the daytime.

Normally, about sixty per cent of the total dose of insulin is given in the morning and about forty per cent before the evening meal. However, your doctor may adjust the dose depending upon your age, weight, dietary habits, etc.

Home monitoring of blood glucose is very important for insulin therapy. Your doctor is likely to recommend that you measure blood glucose level before breakfast, before lunch, before dinner and at bedtime at least twice a week.

Is frequent monitoring of blood sugar levels necessary?

The amount of blood sugar changes throughout the day. If its level rises too high or falls too low, it can lead to serious complications. This is why it is important to measure blood sugar levels several times a day. Self-monitoring of blood glucose is very important in insulin-dependent diabetes. It helps you detect when your blood sugar is too low or too high. It is also important in non-insulin dependent diabetes for making finer adjustments in the medicines, diet or exercise.

When should blood sugar level be tested?

Blood sugar testing is recommended at least three times a day, especially when the dose of insulin and/or medicines is being adjusted. The recommended timings are before meals, at bedtime and one or two hours after meals. Your doctor may also recommend that you check the blood sugar levels at about two in the morning at least once a week. You also need to check blood sugar level when you are sick, have changed the dose or timing of medicines, diet or exercise, or have lost or gained weight and when you suspect low blood sugar.

How is blood sugar level measured?

There are two ways in which you can test your blood to measure the sugar levels. These include testing with strips and with meter. In both these methods, you first need to prick your finger with a special needle to get a drop of blood. The side of the finger is a preferred site for pricking as pain is likely to be less here. Change the sites if you are measuring blood sugar levels several times a day. Some medical professionals recommend that you stimulate blood circulation of the site of prick by massing the skin towards the site. Keep your forearm and hands below the level of the heart.

Testing with strips

After pricking the finger, you need to place a drop of blood on the test strip that contains a chemical compound. Make sure that the finger does not touch the strip and only the blood comes in contact with it. Wait for the test strip to change colour. Match the colour of the test strip with a standard colour chart on the bottle that indicates different levels of blood sugar.

This method is also called visual reading as you need to compare the colour on the strip with that on the standard chart by looking at them.

Testing with meter

There are several types of blood glucose meters available. These are small computerised machines that measure the blood sugar levels. Each of these meters comes with detailed instructions on how to record blood sugar level. You need to put the drop of blood on the test pad and insert the pad into the meter as per the directions given with the instrument. The blood sugar levels will be recorded as number.

How is blood sugar level monitored after starting treatment for diabetes?

There are two common ways in which blood sugar levels are monitored to assess if the diabetes is under control or not. These include (a) frequent measurements of blood glucose and (b) glycosylated haemoglobin testing.

Frequent measurement of blood sugar level

Ideally, blood glucose levels can be monitored four times a day to adjust diet and medicines in order to maintain fasting blood sugar level to as close as 70-120 mg/100 ml of blood as possible. This means measuring blood sugar levels before each meal and at bedtime. It is important that you maintain a diary of these blood sugar level measurements as it will help your doctor adjust your medicines, diet and exercises.

Glycosylated haemoglobin testing

Daily testing of the blood indicates the blood sugar level at the time of testing. They help adjust the dose of medicines and/or exercise routine. The daily testing however does not indicate if there is long-term good control over blood sugar levels. Glycosylated haemoglobin testing is a test that provides an accurate picture of your overall diabetes control.

Mechanism of action

Sugar that is not used for the energy remains in the blood. It attaches itself to haemoglobin, which is a part of the red blood cells that carries oxygen to various parts of the body. This process of attachment of sugar to haemoglobin is called *glycosylation*.

Glycosylated haemoglobin testing measures the amount of sugar that is attached to the haemoglobin in the red blood cells. These cells live in the blood for about four months. This is why this test shows the average of blood sugar for the past several months. This is just as the average run rate of a cricket player is calculated over a period of time.

One of the main advantages of glycosylated haemoglobin is that it is not affected by short-term changes in the blood sugar levels. This is why even if you have high blood sugar level at some time, a good result of this testing will mean that your overall control of diabetes is satisfactory. There are several methods of glycosylated haemoglobin testing. Each of these tests results need to be interpreted differently. The results of

glycosylated haemoglobin testing are normally interpreted as follows:
- Very good control — 6% or 120 mg/100 ml of blood
- Good control — 8% or 180 mg/100 ml of blood
- Poor control — 10% or 240 mg/100 ml of blood
- Dangerous level — 13% or 330 mg/100 ml of blood.

How does diabetes affect the skin?

Detailed below are some of the common skin problems associated with diabetes.

Shin spots

About fifty per cent people with diabetes are likely to have this condition. It results in well-defined brownish scars on the shin. They may also be present on the forearms, thighs and bony prominences. These scars are normally present on both sides of the body and several of them may appear at the same time. Shin spots are more common among men than women.

Redness of the skin

This is because of a disease condition in which there are well-defined patches of red skin on the legs and feet of elderly people. These patches are often due to damage to the underlying bones. Sometimes there may be rosy discolouration of the face, hands and feet because of damage to smaller blood vessels of the skin.

Thickened skin

This is due to damage to the proteins of the skin. This damage may be a natural process of aging but its progress is more rapid among people with diabetes.

About seventy-five per cent people with diabetes who are above sixty years of age are likely to have abnormal skin on the hand with varying severity. Thickened skin on the back of the fingers may adversely affect their movement in the advanced stages. Some people may also develop stiff and painful fingers.

Thickened skin on the back of the neck and upper part of the back is common among people with non-insulin dependent diabetes, especially those who are obese.

White patches

Patchy discolouration of the skin is two times more common among people with insulin dependent diabetes than those without diabetes.

Infections

Bacterial and fungal infections are more common among people with diabetes, especially if the blood sugar levels are not under control. *Diabetes should be suspected in women who have fungal infection of the vagina and external genitalia that does not respond to standard treatment.* These infections result in severe irritation, redness and abnormal white discharge.

Treatment of skin problems in diabetes depend upon their type, severity and whether they adversely affect normal functions of the affected part.

What are the foot problems in diabetes?

Ulcers in the foot, with or without infections and *gangrene*, either localised or involving the whole foot are two main foot problems in diabetes. Ulcers are crater-like wounds in the skin or mucous membrane with a defined edge. They are formed due to damage to the skin or mucous membrane due to several causes such as inflammation, infections, etc. Gangrene is death of some part of the tissue in the body due to loss of blood supply, bacterial infection and subsequent decay of the tissue.

The foot problems in diabetes are due to several reasons. These include, damage to the nerves of the feet, lack of or reduced blood supply and infections.

What is the classification of foot problems in diabetes?

Injury to the foot due to diabetes is normally classified into five grades. This classification is used mainly as a guide for management of foot injuries. Box 17 lists the five grades that are described below.

Grade 0

Anyone with diabetes who has characteristics listed in Box 18 is considered as having high risk of developing ulcers in the foot. Regular care of the feet and check-up by the doctor can prevent foot problems at this stage.

Box 17: Classification of diabetic foot disease

- Grade 0 — High risk of developing foot disease. No ulcers are present.
- Grade 1 — Superficial ulcers that are not infected.
- Grade 2 — Deeper ulcers, often associated with inflammation of the surrounding tissue. No infection of the bones and abscess formation.
- Grade 3 — Deep ulcers with involvement of the bones and formation of abscess.
- Grade 4 — Localised gangrene, such as in the toe, front part of the foot or heel.
- Grade 5 — Gangrene of the whole foot.

Box 18: High risks of developing diabetic foot problems

People with the following characteristics are at a high risk of developing diabetic foot disease:
- Damage to the nerves of the feet.
- Diseases of the blood vessels of the legs.
- Having foot ulcers in the past.
- Deformity of the foot.
- Presence of callus.
- Blind or with poor vision, kidney diseases, especially chronic kidney failure.
- Elderly people, especially those living alone.
- People who cannot reach their feet on their own to clean them.
- Poor control of blood sugar levels, and
- Reduced sensation in the feet.

Grade 1

Superficial ulcers that involve only the upper layer of the skin are classified in this group. At this stage, there is no infection. Normally, these ulcers are because of damage to the nerves, which in turn reduce the sensation in the affected parts. This is why these ulcers are located in sites where there is more weight bearing of the body. For example, lower part of the foot or toes that come in contact with the ground are common sites for these ulcers. Sometimes *callus* tissue may be present. Callus means thickening of a well-defined area of the skin. Occasionally, the callus may hide an ulcer below the thickened area.

Grade 2

This stage includes deep ulcers that penetrate the skin and the underlying tissues. There may be infection of the skin and the tissues below it. Several types of bacteria, some of which are difficult to grow in artificial medium in the laboratory, can cause foot infections in diabetes. There is however no infection in the bones of the foot or *abscess* formation. An abscess is a localised collection of pus surrounded by inflamed tissue.

Grade 3

This is the stage of deep ulcers that often affect the bones. There is also associated infection of deeper tissues of the foot. Abscess formation is common in this stage.

Grade 4

In this stage there is lack of blood supply and therefore gangrene in specific parts of the foot. Nerve damage is often present and may worsen the condition. If nerve damage is present, there will be no pain sensation. Infections are common in the damaged and dead parts of the foot.

Grade 5

This is the stage where there is gangrene of the entire foot because of blocks in any major blood vessel of the foot. Damage to the nerves and infections usually worsen the condition.

What is the management of diabetic foot problems?

The first priority for foot care in people with diabetes is to prevent ulcers in the foot from developing. In case you develop an ulcer, your doctor will first assess whether it is because of damage to the nerves or lack of blood supply or infections. This is because each of these contributory factors requires different types of treatment.

Management of damage to the nerves

Most people with diabetes who have foot problems are likely to have pain, decreased sensation or numbness in the foot. The progress of the nerve damage may however be so slow that you may not even notice these symptoms. Sometimes pain may be absent and therefore development of ulcers may not be noticed in the early stages. Thus, lack of symptoms of nerve damage does not mean that there is no damage. This is why your doctor will first carefully examine your feet, especially the areas where there is increased weight bearing such as heel, lower part of the foot at the end of the toes, etc. Damage to the nerves of the feet may result in signs such as ulcers hidden below the callus skin, warm dry skin, enlarged veins on the skin and reduced sensation.

Normally, laboratory tests are not recommended for diagnosis and management of damaged nerves of the feet. Occasionally, some tests may be required. These include measurements of (a) light touch sensation, (b) sensitivity to temperature; (c) sensation of vibration and (d) efficiency of nerves for transmitting messages to and from the brain. Your doctor is also likely to examine your footwear to ensure that they fit correctly. This is because ill-fitting footwear can also cause ulcers in the foot.

Most ulcers because of damage to the nerves heal satisfactorily with simple measures. Your doctor will recommend that you avoid putting pressure on the affected part of the foot. In case you are not able to rest the foot and avoid weight bearing, your doctor may recommend a plaster of Paris cast or a removable boot that protects the foot just as a plaster cast would. It is important that you go for regular check-ups to ensure that the ulcer is healing. This is because a cast that has not been put correctly may cause further damage to the feet.

Some medical practitioners recommend application of a moist dressing to promote healing while some others believe that removing pressure from the affected foot and ensuring adequate blood circulation is adequate for satisfactory healing of the ulcers.

Management of lack of blood supply

Lack of blood supply to the legs and feet may result in symptoms such as weakness in the legs and cramp-like pain in the calf muscles, thighs or buttocks, pain in the leg even at rest that is often worse at night, etc. Just as the symptoms due to damage to the nerves, these symptoms may also be very mild and you may ignore them. Lack of blood supply may lead to signs such as cold skin, loss of hair and thickening of the nails. Your doctor may find it difficult to feel the pulse in the foot or in the leg.

In order to make an accurate diagnosis and treat you in the most suitable way, your doctor may suggest laboratory tests such as *Doppler ultrasound studies* in the arteries of the legs and foot. Doppler ultrasound studies is a technique in which very high frequency sound waves are used to study the behaviour of moving structures in the body such as blood or heart valves. The types of ultrasound waves that are reflected from a moving surface are different from those reflected from other surfaces.

In case your doctor suspects very severe loss of blood supply or Doppler ultrasound studies indicate any abnormalities, your doctor may recommend *areteriography* of the leg. In this procedure, a chemical substance that shows up on the X-rays is injected into the arteries of the legs and a series of pictures taken. This test is often used to detect blocks in the arteries that may be removed through a balloon attached to the tip of a tube. This tube can be inserted into the affected artery and the balloon inflated at the site of the block. The blood flow therefore returns to normal. If the blood supply is greatly diminished, surgery may be necessary to bypass the blocks in the arteries of the legs and therefore reduce the risk of amputation.

Management of infections in diabetic foot ulcers

It is often difficult to determine the severity of the infections in the ulcers of the foot due to diabetes. It is also difficult to determine if the infection has reached the deeper structures of the leg including the bones. Normally, infection in any injury to the skin leads to redness, pain and painful touch. These symptoms may however be absent in diabetes, especially if there is associated damage to the nerves of the foot. Your doctor is therefore likely to "dig" into the deeper areas of the foot to detect infection in the deeper areas, especially bones, if any. He/she will also look for infection with some bacteria that cause gas formation in the affected part of the foot. Presence of gas in these tissues indicates deep infection that may be difficult to control.

An x-ray is often necessary to determine whether the bones of the foot are also affected or not. Your doctor will also collect some part of the affected foot and send it for *culture sensitivity*. This means that the bacteria from the tissue of your foot will be first isolated and then grown in an artificial medium in the laboratory. Tests will be conducted to identify the most effective antibiotics.

Most people with infections of the foot duet to diabetes require hospital admission, especially if the bones are involved or there is abscess formation. This is because in order to control diabetes, insulin injections may be necessary in relatively higher doses. Also, intravenous injections of a combination of antibiotics are often needed to control the infection.

Treatment options differ for superficial and deep infections. Normally, the most effective antibiotic for controlling the infection is detected only after doing culture sensitivity tests. Superficial ulcers may be treated by oral antibiotics such as amoxycillin-clavulanate or ciprofloxacin with clindamycin. Oral medicines may need to be taken for several weeks for effective control of the infection. Deep infections are also treated with antibiotics that are initially given as intravenous injections and then as oral medicines for several weeks, sometimes even for twelve weeks.

Management of gangrene of the foot

Death of the tissue of the foot, either a part of it or the entire foot is easy to diagnose. Detailed tests are however necessary to study the amount and extent of blood circulation in the legs and the foot. Repair of the

> **Box 19: General guidelines for preventing foot ulcers**
>
> - Inspect your feet every day in order to detect ulcers, if any, at the earliest.
> - Check your shoes both inside and outside before wearing them to detect stones or other similar objects that may be present.
> - Get the feet size measured every time you buy new footwear.
> - Keep the feet away from heat, hot water, etc.
> - Wear protective footwear inside the house also and avoid walking barefoot.
> - Wear shoes that have laces and plenty of space for the toes.

affected portion of the blood vessels in the legs is often recommended for grade 4 of the ulcers. This repair can be done either through an *angioplasty* or bypass surgery. Angioplasty is an invasive procedure in which the blocks in the arteries are removed through "tubes" inserted into it. Bypass surgery is a procedure in which the healthy portion of the artery just above the block is connected with the help of another blood vessel to the artery just below the block. The flow of blood is therefore restored through the bypass. In addition to surgical treatment for the damaged part of the arteries, suitable antibiotics are recommended for control of infections.

People who have gangrene or pain in the foot at rest normally require surgery to remove the affected part. In case of gangrene of the entire foot, amputation of the leg below the knee is often recommended, as healing rarely occurs at a level below that.

Box 19 lists the general guidelines for preventing foot ulcers.

How does sickness affect diabetes control?

Many illnesses including minor diseases can adversely affect blood sugar control. Viral cold, cough, infections, fever, vomiting, diarrhoea or injuries increase the need for insulin. Emotional stress can also affect blood glucose levels. So can surgery. This is why it is important for you to understand when and how to adjust the dose of your insulin and/or medicines. Do not, however, change the dose of your medicines without consulting with your doctor first.

Box 20 lists general guidelines for control of diabetes during illness.

If you have insulin dependent diabetes, your doctor is likely to recommend that you add regular insulin to your normal dose. This will help your body use sugar in the blood and prevent breakdown of the fat cells which can increase the level of ketones in the blood. The additional dose of insulin will depend upon your blood sugar.

In case your blood sugar level is below 150 mg/100ml and you are not able to take normal meals because of illness, nausea, vomiting, etc., your doctor is likely to recommend that you avoid taking regular insulin and take only NPH or Lente insulin in a

Box 20: Guidelines for blood sugar control during sickness

- Do not miss any dose of the insulin. Your dose may vary, depending upon the type and severity of illness.
- Do not take additional oral medicines for diabetes during illness.
- Drink increased volume of water or other clear fluids and eat frequent, light meals.
- Avoid doing any exercise during illness.
- Consult your doctor again if the illness lasts for more than two days, or you have vomiting and diarrhoea for more than four to five hours.
- In case you have insulin dependent diabetes, you need to test your urine every three to four hours for ketones.

modified dose, if necessary. These are intermediate acting insulins.

If you have non-insulin dependent diabetes and you are taking oral medicines, it is important that you watch for symptoms of low blood sugar. Your blood sugar levels are likely to go down especially if you have nausea or vomiting.

It is important that you consume as much carbohydrate as possible. If you are unable to consume normal diet, you can substitute carbohydrates with liquids or soft foods such as khichdi. The carbohydrates will provide the necessary sugar for the body's energy requirements. If you do not consume adequate carbohydrate, the body will burn fat for energy. Burning fat for energy can increase ketones in the blood, which in high levels can be dangerous.

How does diabetes increase the risk of infections?

There are several factors that increase the risk of infections in diabetes. High blood sugar levels provide a good medium for the infectious agents such as bacteria to grow. In addition, it is believed that diabetes alters the functions of the white blood cells, which are responsible for "killing" the disease causing germs.

Detailed below are some of the infections that are common in people with diabetes.

Urinary tract infections

These infections are more common among people with diabetes, especially women. They are more common in older people who have had diabetes for several years. It is also common in people with nerve damage, as a result of which they are unable to empty their bladder completely.

Urinary tract infections may not cause any symptoms, especially if the infection is limited to the bladder. It is however important to treat bladder infection as soon as it is diagnosed even if there are no troublesome symptoms. This is because the infection may not allow good control of blood sugar levels and may also spread upwards to the kidneys.

People with diabetes are likely to need antibiotics for a longer duration than normal people. Your doctor is likely to suggest repetition of urine culture in order to make sure that the infection is completely cured.

Respiratory tract infections

Diabetes increases the risk of getting pneumonia. On the other hand, pneumonia worsens diabetes and may lead to very high levels of ketones in the body, thus requiring emergency treatment at a hospital.

People with diabetes are also more likely to develop tuberculosis as compared to the general population. Treatment schedule for tuberculosis may need to be more intense in people with diabetes. It is important to remember that some medicines recommended for treatment of tuberculosis make the action of diabetes medicines such as sulphonylurea inactive.

Infections of the digestive system

Fungal infections, especially in the angle of the mouth and throat are very common in people with diabetes.

Infections of the bones and soft tissues

Diabetes can lead to a condition called *acute dermal gangrene* in which there is death of the tissue below the skin up to the muscles but not affecting the muscles. The skin too may remain normal in the initial stages of this infection, thus making early diagnosis difficult. Acute dermal gangrene is more common among people who do not have good control over diabetes. Treatment of acute dermal gangrene includes intravenous injections of antibiotics. Surgery is often necessary to clean the dead tissues.

Rare infections and fever

People with diabetes are more likely to develop some rare infections. Sometimes, these infections may not result in typical symptoms. Fever, the cause of which cannot be easily detected, is often the only symptom.

Fever results in dilatation of the blood vessels of the skin in order to control body temperature. The body heat is lost through these dilated blood vessels and the fever therefore comes down. This is why many diabetic people who have high levels of ketones because of infections may not have any fever. Since high ketone levels can be dangerous, it is important to consult your doctor even for minor illnesses.

How does travelling affect blood sugar levels?

Travelling may adversely affect blood sugar control because of changes in the diet, exercise routine and physical activity. You can however maintain good control over your diabetes by taking simple measures that are listed below.

Adequate stock of medicines

Take medicines that can last you for the entire trip as it may be difficult to purchase medicines in newer places.

Glucose monitor

It is desirable that you measure blood sugar levels more frequently while on travel.

Diabetic card

Always carry a diabetic card that lists not only your name and address but also details about your diabetes such as your medications, their dose, etc.

Foot care

You are likely to neglect your feet more while travelling. It is desirable that you check your feet every day and avoid walking in new footwear while travelling.

Time zone

If you are planning a trip across time zones, take snacks and meals while on the flight as per your schedule at the departure point. Resume normal dose of medicines or insulin from the time you arrive at your destination.

How does diabetes affect sexual function in men?

Sexual problems affect up to thirty-five per cent men with diabetes and about fifty-five per cent diabetic men above sixty years. The main problem is inability to achieve or sustain an erection sufficient for sexual intercourse. Milder forms of sexual problems may affect up to seventy-five per cent men with diabetes.

Poor control of diabetes can cause a general feeling of being unwell, which is often accompanied by loss of interest in sexual activities. Fungal infection of the tip of the penis is common among men who do not have good control over their diabetes. This infection may cause discomfort and pain and therefore reduced interest in sexual activities. Anxiety with or without depression is often associated with diabetes. Many people worry excessively about its consequences, treatment problems and complications. Excessive worry about impotence as a complication of diabetes frequently leads to reduced sexual desire.

People with diabetes are more likely to have diseases of the blood vessels such as deposition of fats in the walls of the arteries. When abnormal mass of fat deposits on the blood vessels of the penis, it can lead to inadequate erection. Smaller blood vessels of the penis are also likely to be narrowed or blocked, thereby affecting normal blood supply necessary for erection of the penis.

Poor erection can also be because of damage to the nerves of the penis. Several medicines used for treatment of diabetes and other associated problems such as high blood pressure may also adversely affect sexual function in males.

How are sexual problems due to diabetes managed?

Sexual problems due to diabetes can be managed effectively only if you are able to talk to your doctor freely and frankly, preferably in a relaxed environment. Your doctor will ask you several questions to identify the exact problem. These questions will be related to the following conditions:

Reduced or lack of interest in sex

This condition is often due to anxiety and/or depression. Reassurance and counselling are often adequate. In case of severe anxiety and or loss of interest due to other conditions such as reduced functions of the sexual organs, your doctor will recommend appropriate treatment.

Failure of erection

The management will depend on whether you have complete or partial failure in erection.

Premature ejaculation

This is a condition where ejaculation occurs before sexual satisfaction.

Failure of ejaculation

This is the condition where orgasm can occur without discharge as the semen is ejaculated back in the bladder.

Pain in the penis or other abnormalities

Infection is the most common cause of discomfort or pain.

After discussing your problems, your doctor will be able to detect if the problem is because of psychological reasons or because of any disease in the sexual organs. The symptoms of sexual problems because of psychological causes begin suddenly, may not be present always and spontaneous erections may occur in sleep or while waking up.

In case of sexual problems due to disease in the sexual organs, the symptoms appear gradually, though the problems are present all the time and there is no erection. Depending upon the exact cause of the problem your doctor will recommend a suitable treatment. Some treatment options for inadequate erection include improved control of diabetes, reduce intake of alcohol, withdrawal of medicines that may be causing the problem and treatment of problems of the endocrine glands, if present. Rarely, medicines or surgery to either correct abnormality in the structure of the penis or blood supply may be necessary.

How does diabetes affect sexual function in women?

Irregular menstruation and a condition called *polycystic ovarian syndrome* are more common among women with diabetes as compared to those without it. Polycystic ovarian syndrome is an abnormal condition where there is (a) no ovulation (the process through which an ovum or egg is produced in the ovary), (b) no menstruation, (c) excessive body hair like in a man and (d) inability to conceive. It is associated with insulin resistance, obesity and glucose intolerance. In about forty per cent women who are dependent on insulin for control of diabetes, the insulin requirement changes during menstruation. These changes are believed to be due to changes in the hormones in the body and in the dietary intake.

Weight loss in people with polycystic ovarian syndrome not only improves insulin resistance and glucose tolerance but also reduces production of hormones that cause excessive hair, and can restore ovulation and therefore fertility.

Infections of the vagina are very common among women with diabetes, especially fungal infections. Severe infections may be irritating and painful and therefore interfere with sexual activity. Treatment includes good control over blood sugar levels and medicines such as local creams, pessaries (medicines that are placed inside the vagina), etc., to control the infections.

Can a woman with diabetes have children?

Yes. Most women with diabetes can have children safely but it is important to plan pregnancy. This is because pregnancy may be dangerous in some women with diabetes, especially those who have complications. Also, poor control of diabetes can adversely affect the unborn child. Pregnancy is not recommended for women with diabetes if they have advanced stages of kidney diseases, severe heart disease and severe high blood pressure. The damage to the *retina* in the eye, and therefore loss of vision, is likely to progress more rapidly among pregnant women with diabetes as compared to other women. Most complications of diabetes during pregnancy can be avoided by maintaining good control over blood sugar levels.

Several oral contraceptive medicines are not recommended for women with diabetes and they should therefore be taken only after consulting with your doctor.

How do smoking and alcohol affect diabetes?

Smoking increases the risk of major diseases such as heart diseases and strokes because of damage to the arteries. These can also be the consequence of diabetes. Thus, smoking and diabetes together increase the risk of several major diseases.

Alcohol may delay or adversely affect recovery from low blood sugar by affecting the storage of glycogen in the liver and the release of glucose. Severe low blood sugar because of alcohol intoxication can lead to brain damage and death. Also, excessive alcohol intake can worsen high blood pressure, high cholesterol levels and nerve damage.

Ayurveda

Diabetes is called *Madhumeha* in Ayurveda. Ancient scriptures of Ayurveda describe twenty types of *Prameha*. Some Ayurvedic physicians believe that *Prameha* is very similar to diabetes as described by Allopathy and therefore should be considered the same as diabetes. All the twenty types of *Prameha* finally lead to *Madhumeha*. Some other Ayurvedic physicians consider *Prameha* as twenty different types of disorders or the urinary system. For example:

- *Udakimeha* is considered as diabetes mellitus;
- *Sandhrameha* as *Chyluria* (presence of an alkaline milky liquid in the urine);
- *Sukrameha* as *spermatorrhoea* (involuntary discharge of semen without orgasm);
- *Rakta / Manjishtameha* as Hematuria (presence of blood in the urine);
- Madhumeha as diabetes mellitus;
- *Iksumeha* as glycosuria (presence of glucose in the urine in abnormally large amounts), etc.

The word Prameha is derived from the root *Mih*, which means to pass urine and *Pra*, which means in excess. Thus, Prameha means passing excess of urine. All types of Prameha of long duration, or which continue to be neglected, lead to the condition known as *Madhumeha* or diabetes mellitus. It may also occur independently. In this disease, you will pass sweet urine like honey and your blood sugar level will be higher than normal.

Diabetes is difficult to treat as it leads to many complications. The natural, soft, simple, Ayurvedic remedies cannot often cure it, especially if diabetes starts at younger age. However, Ayurvedic medicines can relieve many side effects and improve the quality of your life.

What are the types of diabetes?

Ayurveda broadly describes three types of diabetes. These include:

Vatika, where vata dosha accumulates in the intestines and travels to the pancreas and adversely affects its function. This type of diabetes is generally considered to be incurable.

Paittika, where pitta dosha accumulates in the small intestines. It initially affects liver and ultimately disturbs the functions of pancreas. This type of diabetes can be controlled with appropriate medicines and lifestyle changes.

Kaphaja, which is due to kapha dosha. This type of diabetes is attributed to *kaphogenic* foods such as excessive intake of sweet-sour-salty (*madhur-amla-lavan*) foods. These foods increase kapha in the last part of the stomach, affect the uppermost part of the duodenum and reduce the efficiency of pancreas. This condition also affects other tissues of the body and results in weight gain. Other symptoms include increased frequency of passing urine, which may be muddy. Ayurvedic literature indicates that this condition can be managed with effective lifestyle changes, balanced diet and medicines.

The three main doshas in Prameha are Kapha, Pitta and Vata, and the affected organs include (1) *medas* or fat tissue, (2) *mamsa* or muscles, (3) *kledam* or blood, semen and other body fluids excluding lymph, (4) *lasika* or lymph, (5) *majja* or bone marrow, (6) *rasa* or plasma and (7) *ojas* or vital essence of the body tissues.

Based on the above description, Sushruta, the ancient Ayurveda surgeon has classified Prameha into two types: (a) hereditary (*kulaja sahaja*) and (b) acquired (*apathyaja*). Similarly, for effective treatment, Charaka, the ancient Ayurvedic physician has classified people with diabetes into two groups: (a) obese (*atishaulya*) and (b) asthenic (*krisha*).

What is the treatment for diabetes?

Ayurveda recommends single medicines, simple preparations, compound preparations and dietary modifications for treatment of diabetes. **Single medicines** include the following:
- Fifteen to thirty millilitres of juice of a leaf of *bilva* (bael — aegle marmelos corr) three times a day.

- Fifteen to thirty millilitres of juice of the stem of *guduchi* (Heart-leaved moonseed — Tinospora cordifolia) three times a day.
- Three to six grams of powder of *madhunasani* (periploca of the woods) with water three times a day.
- Fifteen to thirty millilitres of decoction of juice of the fruits of *karvalleka* (bitter gourd) three times a day.
- Five to ten grams of *swertia chirayita* (chirata powder) three times a day.
- Five to ten grams of powder prepared from equal parts of seeds of *jamun* (black plum), *karvalleka* (bitter gourd), *amba beeja* (mango seeds) and leaves of *gudmar* (periploca of the woods) three times a day.
- Five grams of powder of bark or inner wood of *asana* (terminalia tomentosa) two or three times a day.
- Five grams of powder of *methika* seeds (fenugreek — trigoella foenum graeceum) three times a day.

Simple preparations recommended for management of diabetes include:

- Fourteen to twenty-eight millilitres of fruit juice of *amalaki* (Indian gooseberry) and juice of rhizome of tamarind three times a day.
- Fourteen to twenty-eight millilitres of decoction prepared from equal portions of *triphala*, roots of

barbery, tamarind and *motha* (mustaka) to be taken with three to six grams of rhizome of turmeric twice a day.

- Fourteen to twenty-eight millilitres of decoction prepared from equal portions of barks of *lodhra* and *katphala* (boxmyrtle), fruit rind of *haritaki* (chebulic myrobalan) and root of *mustaka* (motha) to be taken with three to six grams of powdered rhizome of turmeric twice a day.

- Fourteen to twenty-eight millilitres of decoction prepared from equal portions of leaves of *patola* (a variety of small cucumber – snake gourd) and *neem*, fruit rind of *amalaki* (embelic myrobalan) and stem of *guduchi* three times a day.

- Fourteen to twenty-eight millilitres of decoction prepared from equal portions of roots of *manjistha* (madder), *salmala* (Indian cotton tree), *kusa-kasa* (sacred grass) and *danti* (wild croton) and whole plant of *durva* (doob grass) thrice a day.

- Fourteen to twenty-eight millilitres of decoction prepared from equal portions of wood of *devadaru* (deodar), roots of *daruharidra* (barberry) and *mustaka* (motha) and fruit rind of *amalaki* (embelic myrobalan) thrice a day.

- One gram of powder prepared from one part of stem of *sariva* (Indian sarsaparilla), one part of *tejapatra* (tamala leaf), one part of root of *yastimadhu* (glycyrrhiza) with fifty to hundred millilitres of water twice a day.

Compound preparations recommended for diabetes include:
- One to three grams of *narasimha churna* to be taken with hundred to two hundred and fifty millilitres of milk twice a day.
- One gram of *suddha* (purified) *silajatu* to be taken with sufficient honey to make a paste twice a day.
- One or two tablets of *chandraprabha vati* or *shivagutika* to be taken with seven to fourteen millilitres of leaf juice of *bimbi* (scarlet fruited gourd) thrice a day.
- One to two *mamajjaka-ghana vati* to be taken with hundred to two hundred and fifty millilitres of milk thrice a day.
- One hundred and twenty to three hundred and fifty milligrams of *vangesvara rasa* to be taken thrice a day with sufficient to form a paste.
- One vati of *vasanta kusumakara rasa* or *makaradhaja* to be taken thrice a day with sufficient honey to make a paste.
- One hundred and twenty to two hundred and fifty milligrams of *svarna vanga* to be taken with hundred to two hundred and fifty millilitres of milk thrice a day.
- One hundred and twenty to two hundred and fifty milligrams of *vangabhsma* to be taken with one hundred to two hundred and fifty millilitres of milk twice a day.

- One to two pills of *goksuradi* (prameha adhikara) to be taken with one hundred to two hundred and fifty millilitres of milk twice a day.

Foods recommended for management of diabetes include barley seeds, wheat, *kodrava* (a kind of grain), Italian millet, *mudga* (phaselous bean), *kulattha* (dolichos bean) and *adhaki* (Pigeon grain); fruit and leaf of *patola* and *sigru* (horse radish), fruits of *karvellaka* (bitter gourd), *udumbara* (gular-fig), *kapittha* (wood apple) and *jambu*; leaf and stem of *guduchi* and *triphala*.

Foods that you need to avoid in case of diabetes include sour, sweet and excessively salty, freshly harvested grain, rice, sweet drinks, jaggery, curd, excessive ghee and oil.

In addition to the above treatment options and dietary modification, you should also avoid sedentary life, sleeping during the day, suppressing the urge to pass urine and eating excessive food. Control of diabetes and its complications requires medicines, diet and exercise.

Homoeopathy

The definition, signs and symptoms, causes and types of diabetes mellitus as per Homoeopathy are the same as those detailed in the section on Allopathy. Homoeopathic medicines are not recommended for insulin dependent or Type I diabetes.

What is the aim of Homoeopathic treatment for diabetes?

There are three main aims of Homoeopathic treatment for diabetes. These include:
- To control the blood sugar levels;
- To reduce the dose of allopathic medicines for diabetes; and
- Prevent complications of diabetes on other parts of the body such as eyes, kidneys, nerves, etc.

What is the Homoeopathic approach for treatment of diabetes?

Just as for all health problems, a detailed case history forms the basis of management of any disease as per Homoeopathic system of medicine. Your Homoeopath will lay special emphasis on the following before deciding on the medicine and its dose that is most suited to you.

Onset

It is important that you tell your doctor of any physical or mental stress that may have been present when the symptoms first appeared. It is likely that these stresses might have precipitated diabetes. It has been observed that many people in who do not have diabetes in other family members develop the disease after a period of physical illness, fatigue or mental stress such as due to grief, shock, etc.

The stress triggers off a reaction in the body that affects (a) its natural defence mechanism and (b) hormonal functions. As a result, diseases such as diabetes develop. This type of reaction to stress is observed more often in people with Type A personality. Such people are overworked, have a high profile work, are easily stressed, are over anxious or have nervous temperament. They may also be short-tempered and have a dominating character.

Homoeopathy offers a wide range of medicines that are beneficial to such stressed people. These medicines therefore enhance the body's natural defence mechanism and control the disease process.

Family history

As mentioned in the section on Allopathy, diabetes tends to run in families. There are several Homoeopathic medicines that are effective in such cases. These include Thuja, Tuberculinum, Medorrhinum, etc.

Individual symptoms

Your doctor will ask detailed questions regarding your eating habits prior to onset of diabetes, likes and dislikes, digestion, bowel movements, sleep pattern, etc. He/she will lay special emphasis on any unusual, unique or unexpected symptoms as they will facilitate selection of medicines that are most suited to you.

Laboratory investigations

A detailed case-taking is incomplete without laboratory investigations. Your doctor will therefore recommend tests to determine the blood and urine sugar levels.

What is the treatment for diabetes?

There are several Homoeopathic medicines that are specific to diabetes and aim at reducing the blood sugar levels. There are also some other medicines that are deep acting constitutional medicines. These medicines act directly on the defence mechanism of the body and enhance the body's natural ability to fight disease. As a result the root cause of the disease can be eradicated.

Medicines that are commonly used for treatment of non-insulin dependent diabetes include the following:

Syzygium, Jaborandi, Gymnema sylvestre

These three medicines act on the pancreas directly and control blood sugar levels. They also help prevent complications of diabetes.

Uranium nitrate

This medicine controls increased frequency of passing the urine and reduces blood sugar level. It also helps correct associated problems such as improper digestion of food, weakness, lethargy and weight loss despite having increased appetite.

Phosphoric acid

This medicine is recommended for diabetics who have mental stress, grief, anxiety and excessive worries. People with these problems are physically and mentally weak and nervous. They are also more likely to suffer from recurrent boils and pain in the muscles.

Lactic acid

This medicine is recommended for those who have increased frequency of passing the urine that is light yellow in colour and other associated symptoms such as nausea, constipation, dry skin and tongue and pain in the abdomen.

Acetic acid

This medicine is effective for increased thirst, severe weakness and hot, dry skin.

Phosphorus

This medicine is very effective for diabetics whose family members have either tuberculosis or gout. It is especially effective for symptoms such as dryness of the mouth with desire for chilled water, physical restlessness and craving for salty and spicy food. People with such features are more likely to be tall, thin and extremely sensitive, both physically and mentally.

There are several other medicines for diabetes that are recommended on the basis of your symptoms. In addition to medicines, Homoeopathy strongly recommends the following **general measures** for management of diabetes.

Restricted diet

A controlled dietary regimen is extremely important. A nutritionist is the best person to recommend a diet chart for you on the basis of your age, sex, physical activities, existing weight, etc.

Exercises

Regular exercises to maintain normal weight is very important for effective control of diabetes.

Relaxation

A regular routine of relaxation techniques such as yoga, meditation, etc., will help you deal with stress better and maintain normal blood sugar levels.

Nature Care

The definition, signs, symptoms, causes and types of diabetes and its complications as per Nature Cure are the same as those detailed in the section on Allopathy. Nature Cure further opines that treatment of diabetes includes measures to improve functions of the liver and the pancreas.

What is the treatment for diabetes?

Nature Cure recommends four approaches for management of diabetes. These include: (a) dietary modifications; (b) water therapy and mud therapy to improve functions of the pancreas and the liver and to remove toxins from the body; (c) exercises including deep breathing; and (d) change in lifestyle.

Dietary modifications recommended for diabetes include:

- *Regular meals*

Your Nature Cure practitioner is the best person to recommend the type of food and its quantity most suited to you. You can however use the following as a guideline to prepare a diet chart.

Breakfast: It is desirable that breakfast consists of salads and fruits such as guava, papaya, orange, sweet lime, pomegranate, pineapple and pears. You should avoid banana, mango, custard apple and chickoo.

Lunch: It should consist of hundred or hundred and twenty-five grams of rice or three rotis, two hundred grams of steamed vegetables, one cup of dal, fifty grams of leafy vegetables and one cup of curd. You should avoid desserts or fruits during lunch. The main aim of this meal is to consume complex carbohydrates and high fibre foods. This is because complex carbohydrates release sugar in the blood gradually. Also, fibre in the diet helps regulate blood sugar.

Dinner: It should consist of one bowl of vegetable soup, two hundred grams of steamed vegetables, three rotis and one cup of curd.

- *Water and salads*

It is desirable that you drink a total of at least eight to ten glasses of water every day at an interval of two hours. Drinking adequate water will help maintain consistency and quality of blood. You should also increase intake of fresh vegetables that contain high water content. Avoid dry vegetables. Eat larger portions of onions along with raw salads. Bitter salads prepared from chicory, dandelion, endives are very effective for controlling diabetes. Since diabetes is an acidic disease, alkaline foods such as salads and leafy vegetables are recommended.

- *Reduce weight*

Develop a routine of regular exercise such as walking, cycling, swimming, etc.

- *High fibre diet*

Consume larger portions of green leafy vegetables, unpolished cereals, wheat bran, cabbage, celery, raw salads, whole grain cereals and soya beans.

- *Proportion of foods*

It is desirable that you eat up to two hundred grams of cereals, sixty grams of protein and about one to two teaspoon of oil per day. The amount of calories derived from various foods is very important in maintaining regular blood sugar.

- *Foods to be avoided*

Avoid foods such as all flesh foods, coffee, tea, ice cream, biscuits, cakes, aerated drinks and alcohol. You should also avoid white sugar. Late meals, fried foods and high protein diet are also not recommended for diabetes.

- *Drinks*

Drink fresh fruit juices, buttermilk, tender coconut water in between meals instead of beverages. Drinking whey water every day is also beneficial.

Water therapy recommended for diabetes include:

- *Cold water*

Taking bath with cold water increases the rate of all chemical reactions in the body related to absorption and utilisation of nutrients. It therefore increases oxidation of sugar. Weak people should not start having cold water bath suddenly but gradually reduce the temperature of water from hot to warm to lukewarm to cold.

- *Douche*

Nature Cure recommends an alternate douche on the upper part of the abdomen with a stream of bearable hot water for two minutes followed by cold water application for fifteen to twenty seconds with a hose pipe. You need to alternate douche four to five times in one sitting.

Alternate hot and cold water application on the entire body is also helpful as it activates the skin, which is likely to be relatively inactive among diabetics.

- *Abdominal pack*

An abdominal pack taken for an hour at night before going to bed or in the evening improves functions of the liver and pancreas. Abdominal pack should always be taken on an empty stomach.

- *Gastro-hepatic pack*

A pack covering the upper middle and upper right parts of the abdomen taken for forty-five minutes twice a week helps improve functions of the liver and pancreas.

- *Fomentation*

Fomentation of the abdomen for five minutes and application of mud pack is recommend twice a week.

- *Mud pack*

Daily application of mud pack or cold towel pack to the abdomen for twenty minutes in the morning helps control diabetes. Mud pack to the entire body once a week is also recommended.

- *Oil massage*

An oil massage is recommended once a week as it will activate the skin and improve blood circulation to all parts of the body.

- *Sweating treatments*

Steam bath, sauna bath, green leaf pack and full wet sheet pack are recommended once or twice a week.

- *Hip bath*

Cold hip bath for fifteen minutes followed by a brisk walk for half an hour is recommended at least once a day. It is one of the most effective measures for controlling diabetes.

Exercise plays a very important role in controlling diabetes as it helps burn excess sugar, improves functions of various organs of the body and improves blood and nerve supply to all parts of the body. As a result, liver and pancreas functions also improve. Exercises such as brisk walking, jogging and yoga are very effective. It is desirable that you exercise for at least half an hour every day followed by deep breathing. Deep breathing increases the amount of oxygen inhaled by the body and therefore increases utilisation of sugar.

Herbal medicines recommended by Nature Cure include the following:

- Eating one-cup curd with one teaspoonful of fenugreek seeds soaked overnight to be taken on empty stomach every day.
- Taking celery juice everyday on empty stomach early in the morning.
- Bitter gourd juice to be taken every day as the first drink of the day.
- Tea prepared from leaves of walnut trees, french bean pods and alfalfa clover are also recommended.

In addition to the above measures, a regular lifestyle that is in harmony with nature and its principles such as regular dietary timings and regime, exercises help control diabetes and prevent its complications. Medicines cannot be effective until lifestyle changes have been initiated.

Unani

The Unani system of medicine defines diabetes mellitus as a condition in which there is excessive thirst and increased volume and frequency of passing urine. It is caused due to "hot" temperamental derangement of the liver. Unani medicine opines that diseases are believed to be of two types according to their causes. One, whenever any of the four humours is involved, it is called *"Maddi disease"*. The second type is when only the temperament of the organ is affected is called *"Ghair Maddi disease"*. Diabetes is a Ghair Maddi disease in which the temperament of the liver is altered.

The causes that alter the normal temperament of liver are continuous mental tension, anxiety, frustration, anger, fear, weakness of the nervous system and use of excessive hot and cold foods and drinks. These predisposing factors alter the temperament of the liver. This in turn affects the kidney indirectly. As a result, there is increased absorption. Because of the altered temperament of the liver, the food is not properly cooked and converted into humours by the liver. The improperly metabolised humours are excessively absorbed by the kidneys. Increased absorption leads to excessive heat in the kidneys which in turn adversely affects the kidney functions. Increased heat in the kidneys also result in increased absorption of water content by Tabiat (body's natural defense mechanism) to reduce heat, dryness and burning. This results in increased volume of the urine. The retentive power of the kidneys are weakened due to which *"Ratubat"* coming from the kidneys are not retained. This results in increased frequency of passing the urine.

What are the signs, symptoms and treatment of diabetes?

According to Unani system of medicine, diabetes can lead to excessive thirst, frequent passing of the urine, excessive hunger, loss of body weight, tiredness, burning sensation in the palms and soles, constipation, heaviness in the abdomen and back, dryness in the tongue, indigestion, weakness in sex, pain in the abdomen, and giddiness.

Treatment

The main aim of treatment of diabetes as per Unani system of medicine is to restore the normal temperament of the liver. This aim can be achieved through diet, medicines and exercise.

Diet

Cold and moist food is recommended for diabetes. This means that diet that contains excessive sugar or protein should be avoided.

Medicines recommended for diabetes include single medicines and compound medicines. **Single medicines** include Tabasheer, Karela, Jamun, Kashneez, Kateera, Khashkash, Shaznaj, Gulnar, Gurmar, Mastagi, Khurfa Siyah, Gilo, Tukhmkahoo, Gil Armani, Gil Makhtoom, Afsanteen and Juft-Baloot.

Compound medicines recommended for diabetes include Qurs Tabasheer, Safoof Ziabetus, Sharbat Anar, Safoof Khisht, Jawarish Mastagi, Majoon Falasfa, Kushta Qalai and Kushta Baiza Murgh.

Exercise

Unani recommends barefoot walking on the green grass in the morning for control of diabetes. It is desirable to walk as much as possible. A light nap or rest after lunch is desirable but it is important not to sleep immediately after dinner. You should sleep only after two hours of having dinner.